P9-AFK-832
DATE DUE
JAN 0 3 2004
BRODART, CO.
Cat. No. 23-221-003

Hip, Hip, Hooray for Annie McRae!

By Brad Wilcox • Illustrated by Julie Olson

Salt Lake City

First Edition
05 04 03 5 4 3

Published by
Gibbs Smith, Publisher
P.O. Box 667
Layton, Utah 84041

Orders: (1-800) 748-5439

Edited by Suzanne Gibbs Taylor
Designed and produced by FORTHGEAR, Inc.
Printed and bound in China

Library of Congress Cataloging-in-Publication Data

Wilcox, Brad.

Hip, hip, hooray for Annie McRae! / by Brad Wilcox; illustrated by Julie Olson.–1st ed.
p. cm.
Summary: Annie McRae finds that she does not need to depend on other people to make her day a happy one.
ISBN 1-58685-058-X
[1. Happiness–Fiction. 2. Encouragement–Fiction.] I. Olson, Julie, 1976–ill. II. Title.
PZ7.W6452 Hi 2001
[E]–dc 21

2001001370

To Ann McRae and her husband, Garry. Thanks for your friendship.
And to Welsford H. "Gus" Clark, who ought to have an elementary school named after him.

B. W.

To my devoted husband, Rhett, and everyone else who believed in me.

J. H. O.

“Howdy, Mom!” called eight-year-old Annie McRae as she threw off her covers and jumped out of bed. “Howdy, Chestnut,” she said to her stuffed horse. Mom smiled from the doorway while Annie carried Chestnut to his favorite spot by the window so she could make her bed.

“I love the way you take care of your room,” said Mom, and then she cheered as she always did, “Hip, hip, hooray for Annie McRae!”

That put an extra spring in Annie's step as she dressed and danced her way to the kitchen, clicking together the heels of her turquoise-blue cowboy boots every few steps.

“Howdy, Dad!” Annie belted out as she searched through the cereal boxes to find her favorite.

“Good morning,” Dad smiled over the wall of boxes Annie was building on the counter. “What kind of day is it going to be?” he asked playfully.

"It's going to be a rip-roarin', corn-crackin' day," Annie responded. She poured herself a bowl of cereal and didn't spill a drop of milk.

“I love the way you’re so careful,” said Dad, and then he cheered as he always did, “Hip, hip, hooray for Annie McRae!”

That put an extra sparkle in Annie’s smile as she grabbed her backpack and twirled out the door on her way to school.

"Howdy, Mr. Garcia!" Annie shouted as she bounded through the doorway of Room 14. "May I hold the pointer during Big Book today?"

"Absolutely! I love the way you volunteer," said Mr. Garcia, and then he cheered as he always did, "Hip, hip, hooray for Annie McRae!"

That put an extra zing in Annie's swing as she sashayed her way to the closet to hang up her backpack.

"Howdy, Grandma C!" Annie whooped as she arrived home from school and sat down at the piano. "I hope you're in the mood for a concert!" Annie slid forward on the edge of the bench so her boot could reach the "loud" pedal.

"I love the way you practice piano without even being asked," said Grandma C, and then she cheered as she always did, "Hip, hip, hooray for Annie McRae!"

That put an extra forte in Annie's fingers as her hands do-si-doed across the keyboard.

corraL

And that's about how things went every day–until one morning when Annie woke up, moved Chestnut to the window, made her bed, and hollered, "Howdy, Mom." But Mom was in the shower and didn't say a word. Annie put on her turquoise-blue cowboy boots, but she didn't click her heels.

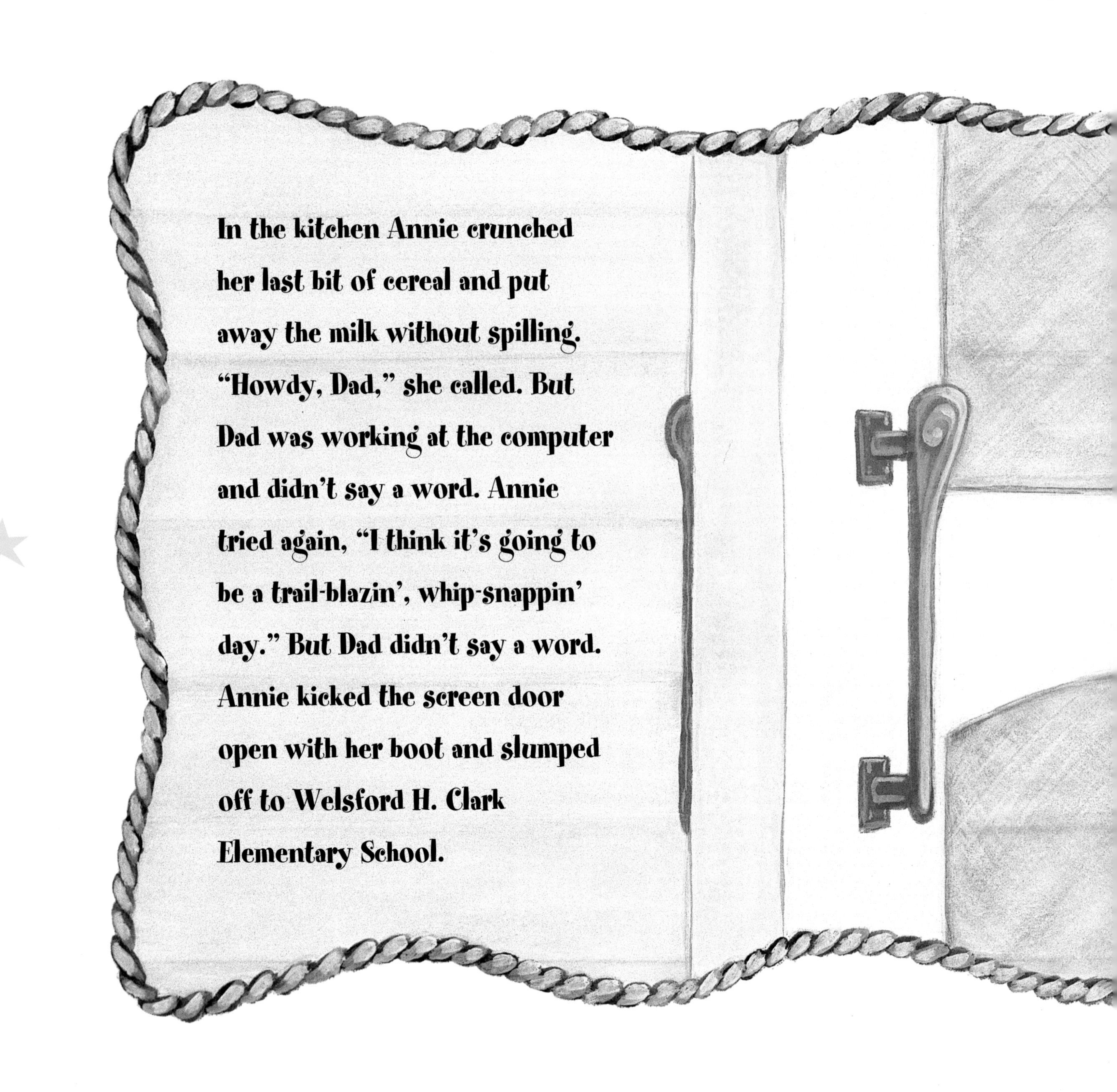

In the kitchen Annie crunched her last bit of cereal and put away the milk without spilling. "Howdy, Dad," she called. But Dad was working at the computer and didn't say a word. Annie tried again, "I think it's going to be a trail-blazin', whip-snappin' day." But Dad didn't say a word. Annie kicked the screen door open with her boot and slumped off to Welsford H. Clark Elementary School.

"Howdy, Mr. Garcia!" Annie yelled. "May I do snap and clap during Word Wall?" But Mr. Garcia was meeting with Whitney's mom and didn't say a word. Annie dragged her boots across the floor and slouched toward the closet.

“Howdy, Grandma C!” Annie bellowed after school as she sank down on the piano bench and banged the keys. But Grandma C was taking a nap. She didn’t say a word. No one cheered “Hip, hip, hooray for Annie McRae” the whole mixed-up day.

Annie drooped outside to the back-porch swing, kicked off her turquoise-blue boots, hugged her knees, and cried till her nose ran.

The following morning Annie made her bed as usual and looked around for her mom. When she didn't see her, Annie picked up Chestnut and moved his mouth open and closed while she cheered to herself, "Hip, hip, hooray for Annie McRae!" Then she put on her turquoise-blue boots and clicked her heels.

At breakfast Dad had already left for work, but Annie was still careful. As she put the milk away in the fridge, she made a deep voice like her father's and cheered, "Hip, hip, hooray for Annie McRae!" That put an extra hip in Annie's hop as she headed off to school.

Mr. Garcia was gone to a workshop, but Annie still volunteered to help in class. Inside her mind she cheered, "Hip, hip, hooray for Annie McRae!" That put an extra zip in Annie's skip as she hurried home, clicking her heels together every few steps.

"Howdy, Grandma C!" Annie called as she sat down to practice piano. But Grandma C didn't have her hearing aids on, so Annie just smiled to herself. She didn't need Grandma C to cheer for her. She didn't need Mom or Dad or Mr. Garcia to cheer for her either. The only one who needed to cheer for Annie was Annie. And with that, she threw back her head and hollered, "Hip, hip, hooray for Annie McRae!"

"What?" asked Grandma C. "What's that you say?"

"Oh, nothing," shouted Annie. "Grandma, how was YOUR day?"